About the Author

Farheen Nawab started writing this novel at the age of twelve and successfully completed it at the age of thirteen. She is an O-Level student at the Bloomfield Hall School, Peshawar, Pakistan. This is her first novel and she wants to continue writing. Some of her favourite authors are Roald Dahl, Rick Riordan and Rachel Renee Russell.

Adventure of BlossomBliss

Farheen Nawab

Adventure of BlossomBliss

Olympia Publishers
London

www.olympiapublishers.com
OLYMPIA PAPERBACK EDITION

Copyright © Farheen Nawab 2024

The right of Farheen Nawab to be identified as author of
this work has been asserted in accordance with sections 77 and 78 of
the Copyright, Designs and Patents Act 1988.

All Rights Reserved

No reproduction, copy or transmission of this publication
may be made without written permission.
No paragraph of this publication may be reproduced,
copied or transmitted save with the written permission of the publisher,
or in accordance with the provisions
of the Copyright Act 1956 (as amended).

Any person who commits any unauthorised act in relation to
this publication may be liable to criminal
prosecution and civil claims for damage.

A CIP catalogue record for this title is
available from the British Library.

ISBN: 978-1-80439-602-5

This is a work of fiction.
Names, characters, places and incidents originate from the writer's
imagination. Any resemblance to actual persons, living or dead, is
purely coincidental.

First Published in 2024

Olympia Publishers
Tallis House
2 Tallis Street
London
EC4Y 0AB

Printed in Great Britain

Dedication

Dedicated to my parents who supported and motivated me throughout. Also, to my English teachers (Farwa, Ayesha and Sabah) who taught me techniques to story writing.

Contents Page

Chapter 1

Life at School and My House

Hi! Are you interested in adventures? Oh, I am used to them now. You may have heard about many adventures but this is the one that took me aback! It was an adventure full of mysteries that had to be solved. Go ahead and read the phenomenal adventure that I experienced.

*

My name is Emella Gem and I'm thirteen years old. Right now, I study in a school and have many friends that are perspicacious in what they do. My best friend is Laura Roll, who has been with me for more than five years. Laura is a pretty outgoing figure with lots of talents. She has fair, wavy hair, brown eyes and a thin nose. She is brave, athletic and an extremely curious person.

I live in a town with a lot of parks where Laura and I usually hang out after school. Laura lives in the same town but in a separate block.

At school, I have my principal 'Miss Helena'. She usually wears pink and gold, has red hair and her identity card has 'BB' and 'Bell' written on it. We would always ask her what that 'BB' meant but we don't know why she never told us. Maybe it was some kind of a family name or something else. Even after being in that school for five years, I haven't figured it out yet.

*

On Friday, when I visited the school, my English teacher gave us an assignment. She told us to write a story about 'A Magical Wand'. The topic seemed fairly unchallenging because I had already dreamt about a magical wand last night. So what I did was quite obvious. I wrote whatever I saw in my dream. I wrote about all the characters and gave it the same setting and plot too.

As I had dreamt about it, I finished writing it in twenty minutes. I stood up and there sat my teacher, moving her black glasses up her nose. As I approached her, she looked up at me from a book she was reading. My teacher firstly didn't believe that I had finished my work so quickly and was bewildered. She said, "Emella?"

"Yes, ma'am?" I replied.

"How can you finish forty minutes' work in twenty minutes?" she asked curiously, fidgeting in her seat.

"Umm… I had the idea from first because I had dreamt about a magical wand last night so I gave it the same story sequence and wrote it quickly," I replied while trying to catch on my words.

"Okay, very well," she said and gave me a detective look. She then blinked multiple times. I tried not to tell her anything else because I felt like I was making her feel a bit disoriented.

After school hours, I went home and waved at my mom, who was struggling with making a messy bun from her red hair, and at my dad, who looked up from the newspaper after I came back home. I dashed to my room and washed my face. I was very exhausted because we had worked a lot at school. I could barely feel my legs so I decided to snack on my lunch later and instead dozed off.

Chapter 2

The Night of Dreams Coming True

Zzzzz… I was sleeping when my mom called, "Emella… Emella? Do you hear me? Come down for lunch." I got quite riled because I remember I slept at 2:30 p.m. and now when I looked at the wall clock, it was 2:35 p.m. Only five minutes of sleep.

Never mind, I scuttled downstairs and inspected the dining table. What drifted away my irritation was the appetizing food placed on the table. The smell of roasted chicken wafted about in the air, making me even more hungry. After I ate lunch, I went out to play in the park. At the park, I met my best friend Laura Roll. I was very contented to see her because now I had someone to spend time with.

"Hello, Laura," I said.

"Hi Emella," she replied. "We met at the perfect time, right?"

"Right," I said.

Laura suddenly got an idea. She told me that because I was there with her, we could play some games. We would play multiple games and at the end, whoever had won the most games would be the winner, of course, and the loser had to get the winner anything they'd like. It was a fun idea so I agreed.

We played lots of games. We played hide and seek, king stop, don't drop the balloon and we also raced. After we played, we added up our points. Unfortunately, my points were less than Laura's and she had won the challenge.

"Laura, what do you want me to buy you?" I asked.

"Huh… nothing," she replied. Her face was expressing fear and anxiety, her face scrunched and her eyebrows narrowed.

I was pretty much not getting what she meant. Maybe she was joking or something? She was my best friend and I knew her really well, even more than others knew her. Whenever she decided to do something, she would, no matter what. We had decided to buy the winner whatever they wanted and now she was saying that she didn't need anything? I was overly befuddled and then me feeling like she was worried about something made me even more confused.

I took a decision myself to buy her crisps because that's what she loved the most, but tomorrow, not today because I had to get home or else my mom would be mad at me.

"Okay then, goodbye," I said.

"Bye," she replied slowly.

As I went home, I completed my homework and went downstairs to eat dinner. I had baked beans with mint, roasted chicken and orange juice.

Now, I was eating…

"Emella!" someone whispered at me.

I asked my mom if it was her but she said no and it was a voice I'd never heard before and I still asked my mom if it was her because I had to make sure it was her.

"Help… come and help!" the voice said.

This voice was echoing around my house and in my head. Only I could hear it, others couldn't. I asked my mom if she could hear it and she said no. I also asked my dad and he scratched his forehead and also said no. When I asked my younger brother if he'd heard something, he called me crazy. I didn't know what was up with him. He gave me a smirk and pulled his tongue out at me.

I thought that during normal, old school days, I was perfectly fine. Nothing mystifying nor something adverse but this time I was feeling like something terrible had happened and that someone was echoing for help and I mean someone was, I felt like.

Besides this, I never knew who was echoing for help or what terrible thing had happened? I guess, I wasn't the only one feeling this because when I met Laura at the park, she was also worried about something. To the hilt, I didn't know if she had the same problem as I did.

The only thing disturbing me now was: Someone echoing for help for something terrible that had happened.

BUT I NEVER KNEW WHAT?

"Emella?" my dad called out.

"Yes, Dad?" I said.

"Is there any problem? You look confused," he asked.

"No. What problem? No, nothing," I said rapidly.

"Well, okay," he said.

I got the feeling that I was being irritated within the environment so I rushed upstairs and went to sleep. I slept early because my brain was going round the bend. I was very exhausted as Laura and I had played a lot at the park.

After a couple of minutes, during sleep, I heard a quavering voice saying, "Emella, I need help."

In my dream, came the park. Over there, Laura and I were walking towards the canteen, when suddenly she fell down and was hurt. After that a construction machine's blaring sound hurt my ears. We ignored that and walked into the canteen. I made every effort to convince her to buy the crisps and finally, she agreed. I asked the cashier if they had them available.

They said, "Sorry, those are finished."

Then I heard a beautiful, serene voice saying, "Wake up… Wake up. You are going to be late for school."

I woke up immediately. I thought deeply about my dreams with extreme concentration and then said to myself, "That's not going to happen, right? Dreams are dreams, not reality!" I stepped out of my bed gallantly, ate breakfast and made my way to my school. On my way, I thought about the dream. It was a dream in which the situations kept on switching continuously. There was no flow in the dream. *Okay whatever*, I thought.

After school, habitually, I went to the park and met Laura.

Now, the weirdest thing happened.

To my surprise, I saw a construction machine that was

building a footpath and its sound was deafening, almost made me deaf. I was astounded because it was a part of my incomprehensible dream. I was kind of okay with it after I thought that it was something normal and I thought that the rest of the things in my dream would not come true.

Laura and I hadn't said a single word to each other since we had come out of the park. Then we entered the canteen; the crisps were unavailable so I bought two drinks. They were placed in glass jars. Laura drank her drink whereas I was left with mine. Only a little bit.

When I got us the drinks, she then started talking. I didn't know why she was silent at that time and now she started talking. She was talking and I was listening to her stories. She went on; this happened, that happened and so on… Laura was so absorbed in her story, so much that she wasn't watching her steps. It was obvious that she would fall and so she did. She hurt herself.

The moment she fell, the drink slipped from my hand and the glass broke into shards. The grip of my hand was completely lost and I was like completely paralysed for a minute or so.

I wasn't shocked that Laura fell down because she wasn't watching her steps because it was obvious. I was shocked because whatever I saw in my dream last night came true.

After coming back from the park, I told my mom about my dreams coming true.

"Mom… Mom… Do you know that the dreams that I had seen last night came true?" I exaggerated.

"Yes, Emella, in which story?" she asked.

"Ha? Mommy, it's not a story. It actually did come true!" I exclaimed. I was forcing my words so much that it felt as if the words had gathered as a crowd in my throat and so it was difficult for me to speak then.

"Dreams are only dreams," she said. "They never come true." I watched her tilt her head towards me with her hair flick sliding to her right eye. I looked away.

My mom was the type of person who believed only what she experienced herself. She never trusted people so easily nor did she fully believe what others said.

She was talking to me in such a way as she thought I was telling her a fantasy story. I also told my dad but he also didn't believe me. Although he didn't show me that he disbelieved, I had inferred it. No one did. And this wasn't happening for the first time. It had, indeed, happened repeatedly. Only I knew that there was something behind this; I knew that there was some mystery behind it and I needed to find out, keeping my curious personality in mind. LET THE ADVENTURE BEGIN…

Chapter 3

I Find the Person Who Has the Same Problem

When my dreams came true, it was evident that my parents wouldn't believe me when I told them because we all know that they don't believe something like this, right?

I myself also couldn't believe it but I had to because it happened in front of my very own eyes. I couldn't just relax. I had to do something! I didn't even know if my dreams coming true were a good or bad sign.

I went upstairs, perched on my bed, took out a paper and a pen and started writing whatever had happened.

First, the construction machine event, then the chips at the shop that weren't present and lastly, Laura falling.

After I jotted them down, I noticed one recurrent thing…

When my dreams were coming true, I think Laura was facing an agonizing pain in her head. She used to hold her head and whisper slowly to herself, "No! Can't happen again! This pain is… augh…" And at the same time, I also felt some kind of an electric current passing through my head. I was dealing with the same pain but I tried not to indicate it.

I wasted my energy and killed a lot of time thinking about my dreams. I needed someone to discuss it with but who? My parents didn't believe me. Eventually, an idea flashed into my brain. "Why not discuss this issue with my esteemed friend 'Laura Roll'?" I told myself.

I decided to tell her because she was the only one who I trusted and then at this point that I thought she might have the same problem. She was the one who always assisted me no matter what. She also used to give me the best recommendations.

The next morning after school, I saw Laura. "Hey Laura," I said. "What are you doing?"

She came charging.

"Hello, Emella," she said. "I was doing nothing, just waiting for you."

"Fine, and why were you waiting for me?" I questioned.

As I asked her this question, she puffed and then said apprehensively, "Ummm… I was waiting for you because I wanted to tell you to meet me at the park today."

I squinted at her and then said, "Really?"

"Yeah, really," she replied back.

"Okay then, meet you after school at the park," I told her.

"Why was Laura behaving so strangely?" I thought to myself.

This time I was sure that there was something erroneous because Laura felt what I felt. I ambled outside of the school and sat on an unoccupied bench. I thought about what had happened lately, kicking the ground and continuously looking down.

Remember, at home, I decided to tell Laura about my problem? But how could I? Every time I met her, her smile faded away and she started to fear, now fear what I didn't quite know. Her face went pale and she started to resist me.

I was sitting on the bench… I stretched my feet, stood up and headed back home, thinking.

As I stepped into my house, the majestic voice came again and it said, "Emella? The park… Remember, Laura told you to do so. Go to the park and disclose your brain-eating secrets. Those dreams."

"Oh yes," I called out loudly.

I hurled my bag and rushed to the park. On my way, I thought, *Is it me that is talking to myself or is it my imagination?*

"It's **true**!" someone exclaimed and I jumped in fright.

I was never afraid of ghosts but the things that were happening were making me believe in ghosts. I also didn't know why I was listening to that voice and doing what it was telling me to do. However, there was something in that voice, making me bound to listen to it and do as it said.

After I reached the park, I saw Laura. I started feeling up… I rushed towards her, sat beside her and said, "Okay, so listen, you girl."

"Yogurt?" she said while giggling.

"No!" I said. "You girl!" I said, irritated.

"Oh okay," she then said.

"Yeah… Lend an ear," I exclaimed quickly.

"I'm listening…" Laura nodded.

I started to tell her, "Okay so… What if I tell you that there is someone who sees dreams and they become reality? This person now doesn't know what to do and is disoriented—"

As I was going to finish saying the word 'disoriented', she interrupted and asked, "Is this true?"

"Yes, it's true!" I exclaimed.

Laura's eyeballs swirled left and right in suspense.

"Go on," she told me.

"Ha? Dreams coming true are freaking *me* out!" I finally told her fervently.

I glimpsed at Laura and her eyes were going to pop out of her head. She stared at me in surprise and then said, "Me too! And I am vexed. I don't know what to do. You said it happened to you and yeah… I am in the same situation. I even called you here so that I could tell you but you told me yourself."

"I thought you might have the same problem as me but to the hilt, I wasn't sure," I remarked.

"Hmm… Do you experience some kind of pain in your head?" Laura asked me.

"Yeah, I used to… not now," I replied.

"Same here," she told me.

We were quiet for some time and then I asked, "Is it okay that we are seeing dreams that are coming true?"

"No idea… I don't know anything. What's happening? This is so mysterious," she said sadly while immediately pushing the fair hair behind her shoulder.

"I think it's a mystery that needs investigation because we both are having the same dreams, same thoughts and pain at the same time. Also, this is not the first time to give us an idea that it's a coincidence. Just can't be a coincidence," I claimed.

"Yes, true." Laura looked down at her black dusty shoes.

"You two, listen," someone called out.

"Laura, you said something?" I asked.

"Na, I didn't." She looked up from her shoes.

"I heard someone say 'you two'!" I exclaimed.

"I also heard something like this and I was going to ask you if it was you?" She chuckled.

"Someone sometimes talks to me slowly in a beautiful slow voice but I don't know whose voice it is. Maybe it is the same person who said 'you two' now?" I said.

Then we heard the same sound once again! It said, "I need help. Please help me! You two will have the same dream and in that, you will find a map. Your task is to find what's on the map. Good luck!"

After we heard the message from *the unknown*, the voice finally slowed down and then finished… For a while, we two were speechless, still and staring at each other when Laura instantly blinked her eyes a few times and glanced here and there quickly and then said, "I am ready to help someone who I don't know."

"I don't know what this person needs but… okay we'll find the map and the items in the map," I announced.

"We adore adventures, right? This is just like an adventure so we'll go home now, dream at night and find tomorrow," Laura explained.

"Absolutely! We do love them. You are right. We'll go home now, dream at night and start the adventure tomorrow," I told her.

"Okay, bye." Laura grinned.

"Bye." I waved and she waved back.

I was thrilled, enraptured and all jumpy for tomorrow's plan! But I didn't know what that adventure was about yet. I did not.

Chapter 4

We Find a Map of Paranormal Weapons

After I reached home, I was knackered. "4:25 p.m." my digital wall clock expressed.

"Emella?" my mom called out.

"Yes, Mom?" I replied.

"Where were you? You usually come back from school at 2:00 p.m." She kept on scratching her neck and narrowing her eyebrows.

"Actually, Laura and I were talking about something important in the park," I replied slowly while stretching my arms.

"Oh, okay but inform me next time about your whereabouts," Mom looked angry.

"Yeah, sure." I beamed.

Mom raised one of her eyebrows at me and walked away. "Pheww…" I took a deep breath and wiped off the sweat from my forehead.

Time passed away like a few seconds. I briskly did everything I had to. Including dinner. I was so keen to dream about the map that I slept early. I dashed upstairs, turned the air conditioner on and hopped into my bed. I was so exhilarated that the rush of adrenaline in my body was faster than anything else.

After a few minutes while in bed, my eyes closed and then a dark place came… I was in my dream now. A dark place, a blue sky with a radiating sun and a broad and tall building with its edges coloured in green. That place also had a colossal playground, some wooden benches and a lot of greenery. Lastly, came a book, some people and then wood. Afterwards, I heard the same voice of the unknown saying, "The rest is left open for you. This dream is implicit. After school, tomorrow, go on and find the map and the items in the map. They'll definitely come in need later… Good luck!"

After this experience, everything disappeared, a black space came into sight and I slept the rest of the night without any other dream. After a few hours, when the sun had risen, I was awakened by my alarm clock, beeping. I woke up and looked at it. "7:10 a.m." It displayed.

"Rise and shine!" I spoke slowly to myself while beaming. I could see the sun's rays shining through the window. I puffed, stepped out of my bed and prepared myself for school. During breakfast, I was eating cereal. While eating, I thought about my dream. I thought, *The dream that I saw was not that clear. At the ending, I saw a book. When it disappeared, I saw some people roaming around in a black background area and when the people also disappeared, I saw some wooden pieces. What could this mean? I thought of it as a clue that I needed to crack with Laura to find the map and the things on the map. If this unknown person needed help for something that I don't know, then why didn't I see the exact location of the map? Why did I get it in a form of a clue?* I pondered over the dream in my mind.

"Emella? What are you thinking?" my mom asked. "You're going to be late for school!"

"Oh, yes. Sorry," I spoke rapidly. "I TOTALLY GOT THIS!" I said confidently in my mind to myself and nodded my head once.

I hastily picked up my bag and rushed to school. As I entered my school, I stopped. I was running and when I entered my school, I instantly stopped. Why? Because I saw something that astounded me. Seriously… I saw the big playground of my school, the huge school building with its edges painted green, the same benches in the playground and when I looked up, I instantly closed my eyes because the sun was shining bright. Everything I saw at school and the place in my dream was the same. I stared in happiness and surprise because I found this place so easily. The place where the map might be.

"So, Mr Map is hiding here," I said slowly so that no one could hear me.

Suddenly, someone put their hand on my shoulder and said, "It's here." I saw Laura raising one of her eyebrows at me and nodding her head twice.

"So, this is our place and we'll crack the code: 'Books, people and wood' after classes," she spoke.

"Yeah… right." I smiled.

After we studied, we were now free and could continue

on our peculiar *adventure*. It was time to leave the school and go back to our comfort zones but for Laura and me, nah… don't expect us to go back home and relaxing. We had to get on with cracking the BPW (Books, People, Wood) clue.

"What in the world could the BPW (Books, People, Wood) clue mean?" I asked curiously.

"I don't know but we have to find out," Laura said while clearing out the sweat from her face with a tissue.

"We got to be organised and do each and everything **step by step,**" I emphasized.

"So, starting off with the basics," I continued. "Firstly Laura, you tell me… Where do you find wood?"

"Umm… Almost everywhere! Like, the trunks of trees, it is also used in the making of furniture: beds, chairs, tables, many furniture, cabinets, shelves, drawers and wood is also used in making trendy and old-fashioned decoration pieces," Laura said, her eyeballs continuously moving from left to right.

"True, yeah…" I said.

"Wait! We know that this map is in our school, right? So, we need to find this wood place in our school, not in the world. This map is not hidden outside the school, it is inside the school, within its borders. So, we need to talk about BPW **inside** our school," Laura spoke while folding her arms and straightening her back.

"Yeah, so like… books, people and wood inside the school?" I spoke while squinting.

"You got it, girl! Yes, that's what I mean." Laura

jumped in happiness.

"We'll find wood. Now we need to know about books and people. Where are they present in the school?" I spoke slowly, looking around.

"So, your turn now. Tell me, Emella, where do you find people in the school?" Laura asked.

"Umm… I find a crowd of people in the playground, in the classrooms, in the sports room, the science laboratory and the library," I replied. "Where do you find books?" I asked her.

"Books in our school are only in the classroom book shelves and the library shelves," Laura said, expressing to me that I had asked her something really obvious.

"So now, let's put them all together," I said. "Wood, people and books. We should consider books in this case because obviously, you can't find books in the playground."

I finished speaking when Laura hopped and said, "So, we only have to investigate the classrooms and the library!"

"Yeah… Oh wow! That was quick," I replied suddenly. I gave her a high five and we continued onwards.

Firstly, we made our way to the classrooms of the whole school. Whenever our classes would finish, we all would make our way to the playground for some fun.

We went inside the classrooms and there laid the tables, the chairs, the clipboards, white boards and some books. We casted around the whole rooms. We looked into each and every space, every corner and every crack but we found… **NOTHING**. There wasn't any place that we hadn't checked but still no identity of the map, no sign no clue.

"Anything?" I asked Laura while catching my breath.

"Nah, not yet." She groaned.

"Umm… Let's leave these classrooms for a while and instead visit the library. It's also our target area, right?" I said.

"Yeah, you're right," Laura said instantly.

"Let's go!" I said excitedly.

We walked towards the library, feeling a bit optimistic. We entered the brown, large, heavy wooden gate with an old-fashioned design. As we walked deep inside, we saw masses of books. We saw the wooden shelves in which laid there the books. We saw some people sitting there, reading. We searched, searched and searched until we were out of energy. Unfortunately, we didn't find the map. We both were so determined that we didn't talk for an hour.

Suddenly, Laura came towards me, charging…

"Yes, what's up?" I asked.

"Emella? Why don't we drink a bit water? I'm thirsty and exhausted right now," she said, panting.

"Okay but where's the water tank?" I questioned.

"At the end of the library, in that corner. You see that?" Laura pointed at a water tank at the end of the library.

"Yep, I see it, let's go," I stated.

On and on we went till the end of the library. I drank water and waited for Laura to drink. Meanwhile, I reclined on a wall. I waited there for her. It was that time when I heard a click. Laura goggled at me, lowering the glass from her mouth and staring out at me.

In the blink of an eye, the wall door opened and I felt

myself lose and fall inside. I fell on the stairs, rolling down into the basement. Laura tossed the glass and followed me. She sprinted from up and followed me.

"Ughhhh…" I groaned in pain. I stood up slowly and watched Laura following me down the stairs, shouting, "Emella, Emella? You okay?"

I tried my best to stand up. I clenched my teeth and tried hard to stand up. When I stood up, I felt dizzy, however, that dizziness was soon to last.

Laura and I caught notice of something. There was a gleam of light coming out from over the stairs, from the basement in the library. It was all dark and all I could catch sight of was something glowing, a box. A golden, shiny, glowing box! I gazed at Laura and she gave me a slow shrug and a questioning look. We ambled till we caught the box in our hands. It felt cool. As I opened it, I saw a map! We had found it! The map we'd been looking for. I touched it and it was made up of thick paper, had a dull yellow colour with battered edges flaking off and it was a bit glossy. We could see some dotted lines pointing to some materials. Laura and I looked keenly at the map and found out that there were weapons like a spear, a bow and arrow and some kind of a stick, looked like a gliss-stick.

My emotions were inexplicable. I was so contented and exhilarated that I gasped several times. Laura did the same thing. We rejoiced. We came out of the basement and jumped with excitement. Laura instructed me to keep the map at my house and that we would start finding the weapons in the map the next day.

On our way home, I told Laura, "Text me after you reach home, okay?"

"Sure, you too," she said hurriedly and I nodded. We both headed home then.

Chapter 5

Locating the Weapons

After I reached home, I had lunch and after that, I quickly ran to my room.

"Reached." I dabbed my laptop's keyboard. "Meet you at the school where we can talk about the map, later," I typed.

"Okay, we will," she replied to me.

At night, after dinner, I turned off the lights and leisurely stepped into my bed. For some reason, I couldn't sleep. I just watched the bright, shining stars in the dark blue sky outside my window and imagined myself on one of the clouds, running… However, that beautiful night scenery made my eyelids heavier and heavier and I suddenly went to sleep. I dreamt about only one thing. It was that same voice and it said, "Everything is clear and evident in the map. Think literally about the map and find the items in it. Quick!"

The following day, it was time to go to school. I woke up early, got ready and rushed to my school. On my way, I met Laura. We both discussed our dreams briefly. Classes also passed. After the classes, some students were in the playground, some in the library and some in the sports area.

Laura and I made our way into the playground, sat on one of the benches and discussed the map. The map was quite clear. It didn't need much inspection.

What we saw was a big tree with an arrow pointing at its roots underground. The second place had my name written on it. I was shocked. I rubbed the wording thrice and it was my name. Beneath it, there was a picture of my room with my study table and there was a tiny cabinet pointing under the carpet. The last and final area had Laura written on it. So, I got to know that it had something to do with her. That area had some stairs and in one of the steps, there was a cabinet too. An arrow was pointing towards it. However, it wasn't clearly shown that at which step it was pointing at. All these three areas were connected to each other by dotted lines, coming from one point and joining at the other till all of them formed a web-like structure.

We both peeked at the map very closely that our heads collided. Laura smiled at me and I remarked confidently, "Easy!"

"Yeah!" Laura mentioned.

I folded the map and made a plan. We decided to look up the clue 'The Tree' first now and the second and third later. "So, the tree…" I whispered. "Where can it be?"

"Let's wander around. Maybe here somewhere?" she said pointing towards an orchard of trees.

"Yes, okay." I nodded.

We were just wandering around the orchard of trees with their branches crooked and pointing up to the sky when suddenly my foot got stuck in a rope tied around one of the trees and I fell down next to a tall, green tree. We both looked at each other and stared and stared. There was a spade lying beside me and there weren't many people in the ground too. So, both of us started digging… I managed to pull out the rope from one of my foot and stood up immediately. I watched Laura go and grab the spade with one of her hands, pulling it across the ground. We both held the spade together.

We dug the ground almost six inches, trying our best to do it secretly. I then spotted something, something lustrous. It had a white glow but its edges were giving off a purple glow. Laura looked at me, gasped with her eyes sticking out and then she started digging at full tilt. Now, we were able to pull it out. I bent down and pulled it out and placed it on the ground to my side. Laura immediately grabbed a white napkin from her bag and placed it on the gliss-stick. We then reformed the ground.

"It's such a pretty gliss-stick!" Laura whispered into my ear. The gliss-stick was about a foot long, it had a purple, glossy colour and it also had a tiny blue button at the bottom of it. I gave Laura a glance and pressed the blue button and it transformed into a decorated pencil.

"Wow!" Laura and I exclaimed at the same time.

"*Clue #1, CRACKED!*" I said with a lot of excitement. "Let's find weapon number 2."

"Yeah, we should visit your house, find the weapon and go to my house and find the last weapon," Laura stated.

"Right," I remarked.

The school bus dropped off Laura and me at the front

of my house. We walked in. Laura greeted my family and we went upstairs into my bedroom. As we entered the room, we placed our backpacks on the floor and followed the map guidelines. The map showed us the study table and beneath the carpet there was a cabinet. Laura and I walked towards my study table and pulled the carpet towards ourselves, outwards. As we pulled the carpet, I found a small space and a handle of the cabinet. I had never seen that before and I didn't even know that there was a cabinet here somewhere in my room. It was shocking for me to see something that I'd never seen before where I'd lived. The cabinet handle had to be pulled outwards. The map also showed the same thing. A cabinet that had to be opened with an arrow pointing outwards.

As I pulled open the cabinet, we found a bow and a case of arrows. It looked ancient but it had a pink colour. The weapon was scratched from different sides and the weapon was wooden. I could feel it when I passed my hand over it. The case of arrows had a floral design with sharp grey arrows. I was examining them, when the same, unknown, soft voice came saying, "They aren't normal weapons but also magical weapons. They have special features too."

"Nice!" I remarked.

"Brilliant!" Laura instantly looked at me with her widened smile.

I also saw something else. There was a small letter with the bow and arrow that said: *"When you shoot and the arrow touches something, it will give out a small, sparkly*

"Okay. So, a small blast can be devastating?" Laura gave out a laugh.

"Yeah… it's *magical*. What do you expect?" I said calmly.

"Okay, let's find the last weapon at my house, shall we?" Laura grinned.

"Yes, but… if I take this weapon along, my mom is definitely going to say, 'What's this, where did you find it, give it back, it's not good for you and you might hurt yourself!' So, now what?" I questioned and Laura's eyeballs moved up instantly and she glanced left and right. She was thinking and thinking deep.

At that same time, I was fidgeting with the bow and arrow… While doing so, I accidently felt like I pressed something, an orange button similar to the one found on the gliss-stick, and the weapon transformed into a handbag. The handbag had a mustard yellow colour, it was easy to carry, it had a steel chain and was gleaming.

"Nice!" I said gladly. When I pressed the same orange button again, it transformed back into the bow and arrow.

"Wow, now your parents are never going to know that the handbag is actually a weapon. Hehe…!" Laura gave out a wicked laugh.

"Yeah, and I adore the bag, it's fabulous!" I remarked.

"Hmm… and the transformation button is the orange one, right?" Laura asked.

"Right! It is. I will also place the pretty pencil we found in this handbag so they'll be easier to carry," I told Laura.

"Now, we need to go to your house and find the last weapon that's in the map," I uttered.

"Okay, here we go…" Laura took a deep breath.

She picked up her school bag and I let my bag stay where it was and we headed to Laura's house. As we entered her house, her mom was standing in front of the telephone.

"Hey, Aunt!" I waved.

"Oh, hi Emella!" She waved back.

"There are the stairs that we saw in the map," Laura whispered close to my ear.

"What about your mom? We need to distract her," I suggested.

"Mom…" Laura called out loudly. "Could you please order a pizza for us?"

"Yeah, sure. Sit down, kids." Laura's mom pointed to the dining table. She herself rushed at the side area of the lounge where laid there the telephone and she called.

"I don't want pizza right now, I want to find the last weapon!" I complained.

"There's nothing to worry about." Laura moved towards the stairs. We looked at the map and it showed us the stairs and a cabinet beneath it.

"We don't know which step has the cabinet?" Laura complained.

"That's all right, we'll find out," I encouraged her.

We searched for five minutes but we didn't find the cabinet. At last, Laura sat down on one of the steps of the stairs to get some rest and she started moving her leg up and down. Meanwhile, I was still searching the same stairs again and again. Laura started swinging her leg. Suddenly, Laura kicked the step of the stair backwards and a small part of the stair smashed inwards. I saw that a space opened. It was actually the cabinet that she'd kicked open.

"Aa aw!" She stared at me. She thought she'd broken the stair step but actually she had solved the last clue. She had opened the cabinet. Wow! I ran towards her and she looked back. There was a vivid shine coming out from the inside. Then it suddenly faded away. There was a long, thin piece of wood. As we bent, we could now see a sharp pointed side of it too. We took it out carefully. It was a long, thin, wooden spear with a pointed edge. It was glossy.

"Yay…!" Laura remarked.

"We cracked all of the clues!" I said excitedly.

"Whoo…! There also must be a transformation button and a note like you also had," Laura said.

Laura shoved her hand into the cabinet and fished out a small note.

She opened it rapidly and started reading:

"This is an extraordinary spear. When the owner of this spear shoots it, a gas will appear that will block the enemy's sight. The person who shoots this will be able to see everything clearly but others won't. A way for others to see is to join hands and the power will transfer from the owner to other people."

When Laura finished reading, she asked, confused, "By

the way, who's our enemy?"

"No idea," I said. I looked at the spear and found a grey button. "Is this the transformation button?" I asked.

Laura pressed it and it transformed into a cupcake. It wasn't edible, of course. It had a lid and it contained 10 more tiny cupcakes inside.

"Wait! There's something else also written too in the letter," I said.

I took the note from Laura and read:

"The cupcake contains 10 more inside that are smoke bombs."

"Good enough!" Laura remarked. She held the big cupcake in her hand and opened its lid, she took out the ten from inside and closed the lid. Then, she clicked the transformation button and transformed the cupcake case into a spear back. Now, she had two things. The spear and the smoke bombs (tiny cupcakes).

"Genius!" I exclaimed.

"Thanks." She went red.

"Where will you keep these things?" I asked. Laura moved towards the cabinet and took out a blue, glossy handbag. It was identical to mine but Laura's had a blue colour. She put the ten tiny smoke bombs inside and she transformed the spear into a cupcake case and she also fitted that inside. Now, both of us were holding handbags not weapons.

"Yes and what to do next?" Laura asked inquisitively.

"Maybe we get another dream tonight?" I replied

doubtfully.

After the discussion, Laura stayed at her place and I headed back home, hoping for an easy yet entertaining adventure further on.

Chapter 6

The Narrow Escape

After having dinner, I dashed upstairs.

The transformed bow and arrow (Mustard yellow handbag) was lying on my study table, with its shiny chain hanging, reflecting off the yellow lamp light. I was thinking about my previous dreams and elaborating them when my brother instantly smashed the door open, turned on the lights, making me flinch and entered the room in his blue T-shirt, black comfy trousers and his hand running through his messy hair. He spoke, "Hey, Emella, wanna watch a movie today?"

"No, Tom, I'm good," I replied back, irritated because of the way he'd smashed the door open and freaked me out!

"We're watching it in the TV lounge," he said quickly, moving the door continuously with his movements.

"Okay, but I don't wanna watch it," I replied, twisting a strand of my hair.

"Fine," he said, turning off the lights and closing the door behind himself. He was gone.

I breathed out loudly and looked at the light rays coming inwards from the bottom of the door. I laid down. Slowly and gradually, my eyes closed shut and I went to sleep. Zzzzz… I went on.

I was in the REM stage of my sleep and started dreaming: *A girl wearing a pink frock, with shimmers all over it. A cloak that was blue, its borders were covered with clear crystals and blue glitters. She had blonde, long, wavy hair but I couldn't see her face. Only a glowing light was sprouting out of her face. She was also wearing a silver, small crown with 'BB' written on it.*

She came nearer and nearer to me in my dream and told me to do something, something eerie. She went on, "I know that this might sound crazy but Laura and you, both of you, have to flee from your own house for some time. Besides the street is the playground in which will stand the big, blue tent. You have to spend some time there. Just carry the handbags (weapons). After spending some time in the tent, you'll see a bridge – 'A Bridge to a New World'. Here your real adventure begins. Good Luck!" Suddenly, everything disappeared and a black space came into view.

I bolted awake with a gasp.

"What!" I said fretfully. *An escape? But... how?* I thought. *How am I supposed to go out now, at this time? What reason should I give them?* I pondered for a reason. It had to be a strong reason or otherwise my plan to escape would fail, obviously. I thought and thought and thought when suddenly an idea clashed into my brain. I thought, *The girl said that I had to escape only for some time so why don't I escape secretly and come back after some time? They'll never know!*

At this point, I was thinking about what a brilliant idea

I'd gotten.

I gradually stepped out of my bed. I looked at my digital clock lying on the side table. So I was escaping at 11:30 p.m.

"How amazing." I rolled my eyes. I thought that I was overthinking. Then, I told myself furiously, "STOP! STOP OVERTHINKING! Get on with it."

Next, I grabbed my yellow bag. I opened my door, snapped the lights shut and tiptoed downstairs, breathing slowly. As I was going to put my foot on the last step, I paused. I crept… hoping for a loud scene from the movie. Like a fight scene or a disaster scene because it contained a lot of noise. And if I opened the door that time, they wouldn't hear me. I peeked at my family from behind the wall. Unfortunately, the movie came into a silent scene and I gasped loudly, "Huhhh…" breathing in. My family looked back instantly and I let out a yell, tripping from the stairs. My family looked at me and then looked away back. Tom was still looking at me with his head tilted and his eyes straight up, right at mine. He was frightening me! The way he was staring at me… oh my God!

"What? Move your rat eyes away!" I whispered loudly and quickly, irritated.

"Okay, you creature," he whispered back. I squinted at him and he finally looked away. Now, all the eyes were focused on the screens whereas my eyes were steady on my parents and on my brother. I proceeded steadily and tiptoed towards the door. I was so foolish… I didn't even watch my step. I was just looking at three people at that time, I didn't watch where I was going. Instead of grabbing the handle of the door, I grabbed the giant glass vase, pulled it and knocked it down on the ground. *CRASH!* It landed rapidly on the ground. I could only see shards of glass on the floor and my heart started beating fast, very fast. "Oh my God! No…" I said anxiously and my family jumped because of the crash. My mom slowed down the volume of the TV but she didn't pause it. I stood there rubbing my hand and scratching the tips of my fingers.

"Emella! What have you done to that expensive vase?" my mom yelled and I could see that anger in her eyes, flashing arrows at me.

"No… I am extremely sorry. I didn't mean to break it. I'm so sorry, Mom," I replied back slowly. She sat down on the floor and looked at it. Then, she stood up. All of them backed away from the sharp, pointy shards and my mom grabbed a broom instantly. She started to wipe out the shards slowly. Finally, when everything was cleared, my mom placed the broom aside and I opened the door slightly.

"Where?" Mom questioned.

"Un…nowhere, Mama," I hesitated. My heart was going to pop out of my chest. As I tried to put my foot outside, my mom pulled me inside. I tried to move out again but she pulled me back again.

"You're not going anywhere! Understand?" Mom got all furious and my dad squinted at me.

"But… I wanna meet Laura, now," I said slowly.

"No," my mom said lightly and I immediately nodded.

When my mom looked away, I tried to escape again but

this time, my exasperating brother got near me and shouted, "Emella is going out again!" I tried to get free but he had held me too tight. Finally, I got free and ran upstairs. Suddenly, the lights went out and I fell on the stairs, hurting my jaw. I paused… My parents ran to switch the UPS lights on. Now, I found this as a golden chance to escape. I crept down the stairs so that they couldn't hear me. I opened the door slightly while my parents were finding the light. I clicked open the door, went outside and closed the door behind me.

"Great!" I told myself and made my way to the park. Even though I was out of breath, I was still running on my way to the park. I ran and ran. Finally, I reached the park and spotted the blue tent. Wow! A smile exploded right across my face, making me forget what had happened earlier.

Chapter 7

Bridge to BlossomBliss

I ran until the short, wooden fence came into view. I climbed over it and I saw the tent lay there.

"OMG!" I whispered loudly. The tent was very beautiful. I had never seen such a prepossessing tent before.

The tent was triangular in shape. It was blue in colour and the lining of the tent was laced with white cotton and tiny, clear stars and snowflakes. The lining was also shining and there were glitters on the borders of the tent.

As I moved closer to the tent, I saw something that shocked me. The tent was actually floating in the air and 'BB' was written on the top of it. I didn't know what 'BB' meant.

"Huhhh… What is BB?" I said loudly and Laura suddenly caught my eye.

"Hi!" She suddenly appeared.

"Oh hello," I said slowly, letting out a gasp.

Laura and I went on admiring the tent and we kept on looking at it. I was circling the tent at that time and she stood there with her hands on her mouth and her eyeballs fixed on the bottom of the tent from where it was floating. We moved inside the tent and our feet dug into the foamy ground. We could barely walk on them. Every step felt like walking on bouncy water with our feet digging into the spongy tent's foam and it pushing our feet back up again. Next, we sat down. Laura had her blue handbag, transformed spear (cupcake pouch) and tiny cupcakes (smoke bombs) and I had mine that was the yellow handbag (transformed bow and arrow) with the pretty pencil (gliss-stick).

"Laura, how did you manage to escape?" I questioned eagerly, wiping out the sweat from my face.

"My family was asleep so it was an easy escape. Ha, ha!" she said haughtily.

"My family was watching a movie, my mom's questions took place, the 'why, when, where,' ones, the electricity was also suspended and I saw that as a perfect chance to escape," I summarised. "I also broke an expensive vase."

"That's bad!" She shook her head and raised her eyebrows at me.

"Emella, I know why we have these weapons. We might come across some monsters or devils but why do we need the gliss-stick?" She shrugged.

"I don't know, maybe it'll come into use later?" I told her and she nodded.

We both felt daring and we waited impatiently for the enchanted bridge to appear to a 'New World'. Time flew away but nothing happened. Suddenly, a bright, white light struck our eyes. Even though we were inside the tent, the high intensity of light would have blinded us if our eyes weren't closed but actually, they were obviously closed.

"What is this?" Laura asked me quickly.

"Please don't ask me. I don't know anything!" I said while rubbing my eyes. Slowly and gradually, the light started to fade away…

I quickly opened my eyes in order to see but when both of us opened our eyes, only tiny diamonds- not real, silver sprinkles and golden-pink powder was in the environment.

"Wow, we're on our way to…" Laura gestured for me to complete.

"A new world," I said instantly. I signalled her to come out of the tent. As we both went out, we gasped at the same time. I was shocked! Laura clenched her blue bag and her fist. What did we see?

We saw the same golden-pink powder but it now covered the whole area. I waved left and right to view what was to be seen ahead. We waved and gradually, the smoke in the air started to decrease. Suddenly, some stairs appeared. They weren't normal stairs. They moved closer to us. Then, I noticed that it was actually a bridge. The stairs were milky white with bright pink edges covered in sprinkles, stars and gloss. I fixed my bag on my shoulder, held it firm and moved closer to what we were seeing. Both of us noticed water in the stairs; water full of gold glitters and tiny gleaming stars. The water was enclosed in each of the stair steps.

"I know that the stairs are worth praising but we need to get on with it. It at least deserves a WOW!" I said slowly.

"Nice!" Laura exclaimed.

As we went closer, a breeze of cool air swept past up, chilling us in the hot days of June. It reminded me of snow. We moved to put our feet on the first step and the cool breeze wafted past us once again and it continued to pass as we took move steps, chilling our faces. I looked at the side and saw the railing of the stairs. I put my hand on it and it was ice-cold. The railing was purple in colour and had shimmery, translucent, white jasmine flowers and bright green leaves. We looked at each other and started to proceed onwards. With every step, the wind would blow and with every step a jasmine flower would bloom. Every step was, indeed, breathtaking…

Now, we were standing on the last step. I looked back and the tent had disappeared by now. There was an arc shape entrance in front of us. It looked as if it was made up of steel, coloured golden and it had creepers all around with colourful flowers. Everything was so vivid. There was a wooden board attached at the top of the arc entrance and it had 'BlossomBliss' written on it.

"Woo! So, we're on our way to BlossomBliss," Laura finally said something and moved forward.

"Yep!" I said excitedly.

"Oh, so then 'BB' printed everywhere we saw, also meant BlossomBliss!" I said quickly and Laura hunched her back and widened her eyes. "Oh yes! It did."

Both of us sprinted inside and suddenly everything disappeared. I squinted to view where we were *and then came a cave type exit… from this world and an entrance to another world.* We went out of the cave and then came a beautiful place. All grass was cut neatly. Flowers of every kind existed there, plants and trees with different kinds of leaves and fruits. The sky was bright blue, the clouds were light pink and purple and glitters were descending slowly from the clouds. They were falling very slowly, in less amounts and they were not easy to see. I could see them because they were reflecting light and giving a glow.

'BlossomBliss,' I read from the board that was hung from the golden gate. I could see inside the same kind of environment that was outside the golden gate. I peeked through the golden gate and I could see everything. The environment outside was also inside, except there were small but excellent houses all the same kind with triangular black roofs and white bricked walls, rivers and grounds with flowers and trees.

"Is this heaven?" Laura was overwhelmed by the beauty. I could tell by her face's expression.

"It's BlossomBliss," I whispered gently.

"Okay and what next?" Laura faced me and asked.

"We need to enter the golden gate, I guess," I said doubtfully.

We went closer to the golden gate and I saw a short note at the side of the gate on the brick wall. There was something printed on a golden template. Laura read, "To enter BlossomBliss, you need to find a gliss. Place it here and then shall open the great golden gates."

"Gliss?" Laura squinted.

"Oh, it's the thing we found under the tree. The pencil — gliss-stick!" I reminded her.

"Oh yeah!" She remembered. "Let's enter it here."

I immediately fished it out of my handbag. I opened the glass case with both of my hands and placed the gliss-stick in the empty space. As I moved my hands back, the glass closed on it and as it was said, the golden gates opened and Laura and I stepped back.

Chapter 8

We Call on the Second Owner of BlossomBliss

"**F**lawless!" we said out loud at the same time, surprised.

Laura and I had never seen something (a place) so adorable before. We moved inside and the golden gates closed gently and made a heavy sound. BlossomBliss didn't look like a limited area. It really looked like a 'New World' because of the vast land. I looked far and still couldn't see any end to it.

We moved deep inside the vast lands of BlossomBliss, talked about how amazing that place was, roamed around and inspected many unusual things.

Then, we saw someone coming towards us. My eyes only caught the sparkles. We spotted a glowing light from that person's face.

Then I said, "It's a girl. She's familiar."

I got to know that who we were watching was a girl because she had long, blonde hair. She was wearing a pink shimmery frock and a blue cloak with crystals.

"Ummm… I think I've seen her somewhere," I said rapidly, looking at Laura who already had her eyes fixed on her.

"In our dream," Laura said calmly then I remembered.

She came nearer and nearer and I saw the silver crown of her head that said 'BB'. Now, I could see her face. She had bright purple eyes, an angular face structure, thin nose and red cherry lips. She stood in front of us and gave us a sweet look but we stood there close to each other, giving her idiotic stares.

"Who the hell are you?" Laura said, surprised.

"Wait." I pulled her arm. I looked at her for a few seconds and then I said, "Hello", not that excited.

"Klora! That's what you say instead of hello at BlossomBliss."

She had the same voice like the one that we used to hear in our dreams. Her voice was light, fragile and I thought of it as sweet.

"Oh, so we've got some rules here too." I nodded, not talking to her with full comfort.

"Not rules. It's just for fun, you know." She moved from side to side.

"Klora!" Laura exclaimed and that girl replied back too, "Klora!"

"Your name… may I ask?" I questioned.

"Oh, I totally forgot to introduce myself. I'm Karolina," she replied. "And… I know both of your names. 'Emella' and 'Laura', right?"

"Yeah, but how?" we both said and stared at each other.

"I know everything. Your dreams, your conversations, about your weapons…" She pointed towards our bags. "Your efforts and the efforts to go on further to come here at 'BB'!"

"Wait. Who are you?" I asked her, narrowing my eyes at her.

"I am the second owner of BlossomBliss. I gave you dreams, clues and motivation to come here."

"Really?" Both of us moved closer to her.

"Yes, literally." Karolina beamed. I had so many questions to ask her but I only asked her some.

"Hey, Karolina… why didn't you give us straightforward explicit dreams that were easy to chase? Our dreams were implicit and we had to crack clues for it," I complained.

She looked at me and then said, "I had to make you people independent so that you couldn't rely on me every time and make decisions and work it out yourself. You people also adore adventures so I wanted to make our journey entertaining."

"Our journey was fun but we had to face some problems sometimes… like the escape." Laura laughed a fake laugh.

"That's okay," Karolina remarked.

She took us around the whole BlossomBliss, showing us all of its beauty, making us admire it even more. Then, I stopped and Laura was still walking with Karolina. Laura asked her some pointless questions like: 'Why are you wearing this and why not something else? Why is your crown silver not golden? Are you an animal or a human?' She was being way too ridiculous. She looked like a three-year-old child who was asking some silly questions that made us laugh. Ha ha!

I asked Karolina, "Does this place belong to you?"

"Ummm… Yes. You can say that but I'm not the real owner of this place. I am the second owner of this place. More like a guard of BlossomBliss," she responded, fixing her silver crown on her head.

"Then who's the real owner of BB?" Laura questioned impatiently, moving to Karolina's right.

Karolina faced Laura and then replied, "Her name is Isabell… she's not in this world. She's present in the normal world – in your world."

"Really?" Laura got all jumpy, and "Yes," was the answer.

I got addled and then said, "Just a second." Both of them looked at me. "Does she know that we're here at BB?"

"Nope, she doesn't," Karolina replied calmly. Laura and I goggled at each other in shock and I was confused.

Chapter 9

Secret of Demon

"**I**s everything okay here?" Laura asked slowly and then instantly gazed at me.

"You people need to know that there is a problem in this place and we all… not only me, we all can sort out that problem together." Karolina gave a smile right after her stressed face expression.

"What are we here for?" I asked suspiciously, folding my arms.

Karolina took a deep breath and then said, "There is never complete peace anywhere."

"What do you mean?" Laura and I asked her.

Karolina then said, "From the past five years, Demon – an evil guy – has made loads of efforts to take over this place and transform it into a place where he can torture people, make them his slaves and make them work for him. This place was mainly made for animals to live because on earth, animals are killed for so many reasons on a large scale. Also for some good people. Isabell, a lady with a golden heart designed this place and completed building it with her superpowers."

Laura and I beamed at each other.

She continued, "There aren't any animals here yet because I've told you that Demon wants to take over this place and if the animals start living here now, Demon might give them more harm than humans could."

I could read her face, she looked very depressed and helpless.

Karolina went on, "Isabell doesn't know about Demon wanting to rule BB. I also don't want her to have knowledge about it too because she might be furious, have a war with him and it might ruin BB. She might start a devastating war that could be treacherous for BB at this point."

We both wrinkled our faces in dejection. "Isabell doesn't know about Demon's secret first and then I persuaded Isabell to visit Earth for some reason only for five years. I also asked her to choose the people she'd like to live here in BlossomBliss. I tried to convince her and so she got convinced after lots of efforts. Now, she's going to return after a week or so and I want this problem to be sorted out soon," Karolina completed and looked down.

"Oh, so this is Demon's secret." Laura raised her eyebrows and gave me a look which told me that we needed to help her.

"It's all right. Don't lose hope we can defeat evil Demon effortlessly with our paranormal weapons," I spoke out loud and clear.

"Yeah, don't… We're here to help." Laura touched Karolina's cloak.

"Thank you, follow me. I've got something to show you. Something fascinating!" Karolina finally looked up and cheered. We followed her.

Chapter 10

Library of BB. History

We headed on and on till a magical space that was risen from the ground came into view. It was a square-type entrance and it had a purple light coming out from the inside. It looked like a teleporting door to me. The teleporting door had a medium-sized board that said 'Enter the Library of BB. History'.

"Oh, so we're supposed to enter the Library of BlossomBliss's history!" I said, all jumpy.

"Yeah." Karolina moved on with her cloak touching the grass and absorbing the dew. I had loved a library with millions of books since I was a kid. I remember myself, really young, sitting in a couch in a library with a book in my hand and then looking up at all those storeys filled with different coloured books.

Laura got over hyper. She started speaking quickly, she started jumping and was the first one to enter the teleporting door. As we all entered it, we exited through the same door but into another place in BlossomBliss. It was an area for only a huge library to fit. The area was made up of clear, strong glass with water under it. We walked forward and saw a huge, square shaped mansion made up of wood with an ancient design. I looked up and the mansion read 'Library of BB. History'. We went further closer and Karolina carefully opened the door with a bit of force and then exhaled. The door was almost five times the size of Karolina's. She opened the door and… Oh my God, the first thing I saw were millions of books.

"Wow!" Laura remarked.

"Outstanding!" I spoke loudly with excitement.

"Come in." Karolina gestured for us to follow on.

We dived in and I saw shiny floors, roof with posh lights and lamps hanging, different colour thick books and it was a four-storey library which was connected by spiral stairs.

"How much time did it take to build this?" I asked inquisitively.

"It took a year or so." Karolina rubbed her face twice.

"Oh wow, that's long," Laura groaned.

"The days here pass more quickly than the days on Earth," Karolina said quickly.

"Oh, so when we go back home, we will be only a few minutes late?" Laura asked.

"Exactly," Karolina replied.

"That's awesome!" We both looked at each other, gleeful.

Karolina rushed and picked up a yellow, thick book from inside that said: 'What Demon Has Thought?', another book that was titled with: 'Evil Demon' and the last book that said: 'The Need to Finish Demon'.

"These books really show us that BB needs help." I

looked at Karolina gloomily.

"Yes, it is," Laura remarked.

"Hmmm… but I have the support of you two." Karolina beamed and both of us laughed.

Laura and I felt adventurous so we both explored the library. I toured the whole library. It made me feel good, reminding me of my childhood. After we were done with our exploring, we came back to Karolina and I wanted to know how to call Demon here at BlossomBliss. So, I asked Karolina how we could call him and she said that we didn't need to call him here and that he would visit BB after every three days, warning Karolina of his threat that he would take over BlossomBliss soon, once he had his powers back.

"Wait, the thing about power? Demon said, 'Once I have my powers back.' So were they lost or what?" Laura questioned.

"He actually was seriously injured when he had a fight with one of his enemies regarding the takeover of BB and concerns regards its ownership. From that time, he lost his powers temporarily and will get them after sometime. But he keeps on arriving and keeps on telling me that he'll take over BB soon," Karolina replied, facing Laura and then looking at me.

"Oh, so he's already been in a fight," I said.

"Yeah, after his powers come back maybe after a month, he'll come here and take over all the land," Karolina stated, expressionless at that time.

"No! Now, we're here, right? We'll defeat demon before his powers come back," I said loudly.

"Yes, and it'll also be easy for us to defeat him without his powers," Laura added.

I faced Karolina and then asked her, "You said that he comes here at BB after every three days so when was the last time he came here?"

"It was two days ago he's going to come back tomorrow and we need to find a way to defeat him." Karolina got jittery.

Laura and I too looked at each other, surprised and started to worry. She literally said 'tomorrow'.

"Calm down! We have today's night," I consoled her, ignoring my inner feelings of minor fear.

Now we planned that we would go back to the main area of BB where we came from and that we would set up a tent there where we could plan on defeating Demon.

We came out of the Library of BB. History and there was the teleporting door. We entered it and came out of it into the main entrance of BB, into the golden gate and we were there! Karolina said an incantation and then came the same blue tent in which Laura and I stayed before entering BlossomBliss.

"So tonight, we stay here in this tent and plan," Karolina stated.

"Perfect!" Laura and I accepted.

Chapter 11

The Night Before the War

The shiny, bright sun settled and the night with a dark blue sky and millions of tiny gleaming stars arrived. We settled inside the tent that Karolina had created. We sat down and planned in detail. We made maps and wrote how we could defeat Demon but unfortunately the plan didn't work out. All of us tried to make up one that could help but none of it was useful to us. We tried and tried, we stayed up till midnight trying to get to an idea that could work against him but when we tried to understand it and think from Demon's point of view, the plan seemed to have failed. Making a scheme to defeat Demon wasn't an effortless work to carry out. Our plans said, "Laura could be here and that I was to be there and shoot Demon and Karolina would distract him." It looked quite useless. Laura and Karolina were trying to make up a scheme; they were absorbed in their thinking, when I came up with an excellent one.

"Demon will arrive tomorrow, right?" I spoke.

"Right." Both of them looked at me.

"So why don't we do something… a brilliant thing." I stood up in elation.

"What?" Laura asked me fixedly and Karolina stared

right into my eyes.

I cleared my throat, I let both of them calm down a bit and then I spoke, "Listen… listen… Laura has two things, the smoke bombs that creates a smoke and the spear that's the same thing. It blocked the enemy's sight. When the owner shoots it, he or she will be able to see but others won't, so for us to see, we have to hold hands."

"Yeah so?" Karolina said quickly.

I continued, "Laura can hide in the big bush that is about ten metres away from the golden gate entrance. She should aim at Demon, shoot the spear, then shoot the smoke bomb for a further distraction and he won't be able to see. We will be able to see because we will hold hands together."

"How will we hold hands if I will hide in the bush?" Laura asked sharply.

Karolina shifted her looks to Laura. "So, you hide in the big bush, I will crouch and be near to the bush so that I can hold your hand and Emella will be there standing, holding my hand too so it will create a path for the power to pass from one person to the other and all of us will be able to see except evil Demon!" she explained my point to Laura.

"Oh, okay. I got you!" Laura rejoiced.

I went further, "So… Laura will be there in the bush, aiming at Demon. Karolina will talk to him. I will be there watching. You…" I pointed at Karolina. "You will ask him if he wants to change his mind and be a better person. If he regrets, Laura will aim at him, shoot the spear and the smoke bombs and we all will be able to see except him."

"I know he's not going to change. He hasn't changed from the past five years and he also had a fight with his enemy where he temporarily lost his powers. After all this too, he didn't change," Karolina said gloomily.

"We'll still ask him once if he wants to be a better person and if not…" Laura said confidently.

"Till now we only have planned how we can block Demon's sight but how will we finish him?" Laura asked.

I paused to take a breath, keeping in mind how long I'd talked and then said, "Hold on… I have a bow and arrow." Both of them nodded. I continued, "It's transformed form is a handbag. I'll be wearing that and as soon as Demon's sight will be blocked, I will change it into a bow and arrow, aim at Demon then shoot."

"Oh, it will create a small blast that can be devastating, remember?" Laura jumped up and down in excitement.

"Yeah, and it also won't harm BlossomBliss because it is only a *small* blast but devastating," I said slowly with a lot of expressions.

"It's within limits, yes," Karolina added.

"The summary is that: We all will be at the bush area and only Laura will hide because she's the first one to take the step. She'll shoot the spear and the smoke bombs and when Demon won't be able to see, Emella will aim and shoot the arrow right near Demon. It will create a small but devastating blast that will finish him," Karolina said and then she asked us if she was right.

"Yes, a hundred percent!" I cheered and Laura nodded her head while chuckling.

"So… are we done with the brain-eating planning?" Laura asked. She looked exhausted.

"Yes," both of us said.

"The only thing left is to defeat Demon and let's hope our plan works…" I said.

By now, we were done with almost everything. We were done with cracking the clues, reaching BlossomBliss, knowing about the person who used to send us dreams and speak to us, knowing about Demon, his secret and making a scheme to defeat him. The only one thing left was to defeat Demon and it looked easy to do so after we had planned it in great detail.

We were prepared to sleep by now. Laura and Karolina just slept in a few minutes and it really looked like they were knackered. I looked out of the tent's cotton made window to the dark blue sky, the shining stars and the huge, bumpy moon.

I was super excited to defeat Demon tomorrow! But I had to accept that that excitement coupled with a feeling of slight stress too.

Chapter 12

Demon's Crushing Defeat

Next morning, the birds started chirping and the beauty of BlossomBliss came into view once again. We woke up and had the special 'BBB'. It was the special 'BlossomBliss Breakfast!' Karolina guided us to an area under a vast canopy of green trees with brown thick bark. Under it was a round wooden table with three chairs for us. The special BBB contained juice of apples straight from the trees of BB, full fried scrambled eggs with mint and pepper and some freshwater from BB's streams. Also the blood-red cherries from the tall trees of BB. It tasted the same as the food on Earth, however, the flavour was more intense. Laura and I really loved what we had eaten and praised it.

"It was my pleasure that you loved the special 'BBB'!" Karolina told us.

"Yeah, we surely did," we both said repeatedly.

"Okay, now, let's prepare ourselves to defeat Demon." Karolina stood up.

"Isn't it too early? When is he going to come?" Laura asked.

"Laura, it's 8:50 a.m. and Demon will arrive at 9:00 a.m.," Karolina spoke hurriedly.

"After ten minutes?" I exaggerated.

"Yeah, come on… chop chop." She clapped.

"Where do you know the time from?" I questioned while looking around.

"There is a sundial that is far and only I and the real owner of BB can view it," she replied.

"Oh, so that's the case," I said.

We all got up the wooden table, rushed into the tent to pick up our weapons and sat down with the big, green bush that was a few metres away from BB's entrance. Laura took out some of her smoke bombs and the zipper cupcake pouch from her blue handbag. She transformed the pouch into the spear and there were her smoke bombs on the ground. I got my handbag. Laura hid in the bushes, Karolina held her hand firmly and I held Karolina's hand too.

"Time?" I asked impatiently.

"9:05 a.m.," Karolina replied.

"Oh, my heart beat… it's increasing!" Laura frowned.

"We can do this, right?" Karolina spoke.

"Right…" I said slowly.

"9:09 a.m.," Karolina stated and I took a deep breath. By then, I couldn't see Laura that clearly because she'd hidden herself so well. "9:10 a.m.," Karolina called out. She opened the golden gates with another incantation this time.

We held hands tight and suddenly, the sky darkened… The vivid colours in BB started to fade away. Everything turned black and white. I was a bit nervous but Karolina told me that it was normal to be nervous and that the changing of the surrounding would take place all the time once Demon would arrive. The dust entered my nose and it made me feel ill. Laura coughed and all of us stopped breathing for a while. Laura had started sneezing and coughing. We looked at the golden gate entrance that had turned grey and we saw a person on a black cloud, entering…

The cloud was about half a metre above the ground. A person was standing on the top of the cloud. He wasn't walking, the cloud was the only thing moving and he was standing on it. That man was wearing a long, black hood. He had gnarled, long fingers and sharp, long nails. He moved to take off the hood cap off his head. As he removed the hood's cap off his head, I saw his long, black, straight shiny hair. His small, green eyes were the only bright colour I could see in him. He had a long, uneven pointy nose. He grinned at us and I saw his big mouth with pale yellow crooked teeth.

I peeked at Karolina and she was staring furiously at him.

"Is this Demon?" I whispered into her ear.

"Yes," she replied forcibly.

Demon came closer to us and he said with his gruff, heavy voice, "Demon the great is here!"

We looked at each other.

"How's he great? He's so hideous," Laura whispered from inside the bush.

"Oh Laura, keep quiet!" I whispered loudly for her to hear.

"Wait, how does this freak have so excellent hair and I

don't?" Laura said again in the same volume.

"Oh my God! Laura… You have great hair now please," Karolina replied slowly.

"Which shampoo does he dump onto his dirty head?" Laura said angrily.

"Ughhh…" I groaned.

"Oops! Sorry," she said, simpering.

Demon was now standing a few metres away from us and he spoke loudly, "So, Karolina… Now you've also got a friend here?" He pointed towards me.

"Why do you want to rule over BlossomBliss? What will evilness ever give you in life?" I asked him politely.

"Oh, you shut up, rat brain," he bellowed.

"That's rude!" Karolina snapped.

Demon backed away and gave out an evil laugh. "He he he he…" He kept on being rude and he kept on saying that he would take over BB once his powers restored. We tried to tolerate all that he said. We all got furious and Laura wanted to come out of the bush and beat him. She wanted to have a physical fight with Demon but Karolina discouraged that. Instead, she considered using our weapons as the best and only way to defeat him.

He turned his face away from us while sniggering. Karolina thought it was a golden chance to take an action and so she gestured for Laura to throw the smoke bombs at him one after another. She accepted and threw some of them towards Demon. It created a blue, shiny, heavy smoke. I beamed and raised my head up. I could see Demon but he couldn't see us. He cried, "Who did this? Why can't I see anything?"

"This is nothing. Wait for it," I said out loud. I raised my handbag, transformed it into the bow and arrow and aimed at him. I asked him, "Do you want to become a better person? I have my bow and arrow in my hand and I can finish you any moment! So, what's on mind?"

"I'll never become a better person even if someone wants to kill me!" he snapped, waving his arms in the air and making an effort to see through the dense smoke.

"Okay then, you'll die. Do you want to become a better person?" I asked him again hopping for an answer that could gladden all of us but he refused again, "NO!"

"Oh, I don't even have my powers to fight against you. Oh, no!" he shouted out loud.

"Yeah! That's great. Do you want to change your mind?" I asked.

"Never!" he shouted.

I looked at Karolina and she signalled me to take that deadly step. I took a deep breath and shot the arrow right near him. It created a black and golden shimmery smoke and I heard Demon yell out a cry. The blast was small. It took place in a small space but it was deadly. I could see Demon lying on the ground with his arms and legs spread out. After a few seconds, all the smoke had disappeared, Demon's body gradually changed into dust and blew away and no damage was caused to BlossomBliss and to us too! Only Demon was defeated and that was the biggest victory in the history of BB! Everything was back to normal. The black and white colours also changed into colourful ones one again. The beauty of BB was renewed. Laura came out of the bushes.

"I can't believe we did this!" Laura cheered.

"We just did it!" Karolina jumped in happiness and I finally smiled.

"Perfect!" I rejoiced.

I could see tears of joy in her purple eyes. She was actually really glad after what we'd done to save BB. She thanked us. We also liked the adventure after all those clue crackings, mystery solving, the tour of the Library of BB. History and now that the most important thing was done, we were more than happy.

Laura asked how easy it was to defeat Demon and Karolina told her that it was easy after all that we'd planned yesterday at night and all the brain-racking which indeed paid off. We could see the result.

"I want you guys to find the real owner of BB now," Karolina told us and we both looked at each other.

"We know her. She is Isabell," Laura said quickly.

"She is on Earth. If you find her, you'll be surprised by who she really is…" Karolina beamed.

"Any clues?" I asked.

"Yes. You need to find out what, 'School, Bell and Peak of School means.' This is the clue," Karolina spoke.

"Okay but not today. Tomorrow maybe," Laura said. She looked really tired by the way she was walking.

"Yeah, that's your choice," Karolina said.

After this conversation, both of us left our weapons behind, waved at Karolina and left off from the cave-type entrance from where we'd come from. We entered it and everything was dark now. We could see nothing and then suddenly a bright white came into view, making us shut our eyes.

Now, we were back on Earth. In the same park.

"We should go back home," I said.

"Yes," Laura replied.

I headed back home, knocked the door and my mom opened it for me. I entered it and I said, "Mom, I told you that I'll be back after sometime."

"Yes, ummm…" My mom was confused, rubbing her face, and her forehead was wrinkled. I tilted my head, smiled at her and immediately headed to my room. I got ready, hopped into my bed and closed my eyes.

That night I had the clue: 'SBP' that was 'School, Bell, Peak of School'.

Chapter 13

Locating the Real Owner of BB

The following day, I woke up and got ready for my school and got there in time. I met Laura in my classroom. Our first lesson was English. Our English teacher – 'Miss Olivia' – told us to write a descriptive writing about an imaginative place.

There was only one magical place that Laura and I had visited together and no one on Earth knew about it except Laura, me and the real owner of BlossomBliss. No one had an idea of such a place that existed in reality. Laura and I decided to write about BB and gave our writings a title that said, **'BlossomBliss'**.

We wrote about the same cave from which we entered, the same setting, the special BBB (BlossomBliss Breakfast), about evil Demon and about Karolina. In our writings, we didn't show that we really had a trip to BB but we tried to show that all this was an imagination because it would be perfect if no one knew about a place like BlossomBliss.

After completing our work, I whispered to Laura, "Laura, a part of the clue said, 'Peak of School.' So…"

She interrupted me and said, "Peak is also the top of a

mountain so the peak of school also means the top of school. It can't be a place because we have to find a person, not a place."

"The clue is 'School, Bell and Peak of School,' so the person is located here in school and we know that. Peak of school means head of school and…" I whispered slowly.

Laura interrupted again and said, "Bell? I saw 'Bell' and 'BB' written on our principal Miss Helena's name tag. It was written at the side of her name tag."

"Oh, yes. I know that. So, is she the real owner of BlossomBliss?" I asked.

"Maybe?" Laura thought.

"We'll find out later," I told her.

Laura and I were whispering when our teacher looked at us through the thick lens of her glasses.

After our conversation, Miss Olivia said out loud, "Your writings are going to be rechecked by the head of school, that is your principal 'Miss Helena', so attempt it well." We all nodded.

"If Miss Helena checks our writings and if she's the real owner of BB, then she'll call us to meet her. And if she's not the real owner of BB, then she'll think that our writings are actually a made-up story," I whispered to Laura.

"Yep," she responded a bit loudly.

After everyone was done with their work, our classwork was sent to the principal's office. After some time, our principal herself entered our class and she needed to have a word with Laura and me. We both looked at each other and gave each other a side smile.

"Both of you may go," Miss Olivia said.

We headed to the principal's office. We reached her office which looked more like a square, wooden cottage. The office had a small pinboard with 'Miss Helena – The Head' written on it. We entered the office and both of us saw her sitting on a red office chair with her bright red hair, golden-pink coat and "BB" + "Bell" written on her name tag below 'Miss Helena'.

"Laura, look BB and Bell!" I said excitedly.

"Yeah, let's enter," Laura responded.

"Should we tell her that we think that she's the real owner of BB?" I asked.

"No, we'll see why she called us here?" Laura replied.

We entered and Miss Helena requested us to have a seat. She took a deep breath and then she told us with her crystal clear, high-pitched voice, "I read your writings and it is identical to the place where I belong. I can tell you this because Karolina told me how you defeated Demon. Gosh! I never even had the idea of Demon wanting to rule over BB."

Laura and I looked at each other, totally surprised that we'd met the real owner of BB. We stared at each other for which went on for a few seconds. "She's her!" Both of us said at the same time and Miss Helena cleared her throat.

"Are you the real owner of BlossomBliss? You are, right?" I asked.

"Now that you people know about BB so yes, I am the real owner of BB." She smiled, swinging in her chair.

"Oh my God! We also figured out the last clue." I

jumped up high in happiness.

"Wow!" Laura said slowly.

"Thank you so much. You people really helped me," Helena said.

"It was more like an adventure for us," I said happily.

"Ha ha ha ha…" She laughed.

"One question remains…" I said.

"What?" Laura asked.

"What's Bell written on your name tag?" I asked Helena.

"Oh, actually, I am called Isabell at BlossomBliss," Helena responded.

So, we figured out that she also had a different name at BB. Wow!

Chapter 14

Award from the Real Owner of BB

Isabell looked at us with her huge, sparkly, brown eyes and said, "What do you want as a reward? You people have done more than I thought you could have done."

"No, we don't want anything," Laura and I answered.

"The biggest gift for us was that Karolina gave us a chance to go through a phenomenal adventure and we adore adventures!" I exclaimed.

"Yes. We truly loved it!" Laura remarked.

"I see… you people didn't know that you had to defeat an evil person like Demon. Now, you did, so you deserve a present," Isabell told us calmly.

"Ummm… You insist so okay then," Laura said finally.

"Right, Emella?" Laura looked at me and spoke loudly.

"Okay, I guess," I said rapidly.

Isabell fidgeted in her seat, moved towards us and then spoke peacefully, "So, what do you people want?"

"We don't know. Anything that you can give us," Laura replied.

"Yeah, anything you want us to have," I responded too. Isabell thought for a moment and then finally said,

"Why don't you people hold up a high rank at BB like the way Karolina has?"

After hearing this, Laura and I were stunned! We were super excited to hold up a high rank at BlossomBliss but then I thought of something that didn't make me accept the high rank. What was so important that it didn't make me accept it? It was that: If we had a high rank at BB like Karolina's then we would always think about BB. It would be hard for us to concentrate on our studies, especially during exam days. So, that's why I couldn't accept it. Laura said the same thing.

"Isabell, I am so sorry for my decision to decline your request to occupy a high rank at BB—"

I was speaking when Laura suddenly interrupted while saying, "Yes… it's due to our schoolwork. Those studies and exams so we won't be able to hold a high rank at BlossomBliss. So, we're sorry."

"Okay, if you don't need a high rank, then I'll give you something else. If you look at it while using it, you'll relive the time of your adventure to BlossomBliss," Isabell spoke.

"Oh really? That will be the perfect gift ever," Laura remarked.

"Wow! What is it then?" I asked inquisitively.

Isabell looked up and suddenly a black space appeared. Golden and pink glitters and a blue gleaming light came into view. "Wait and watch…" she spoke and Laura and I moved closer to her. We watched and out of the black space appeared two gleaming pink and golden metal pens with a floral design and 'BB' was written on them. The shape was like other normal pens but the colours were pink and golden, the design was floral and bells were hanging from the flowers, they were shining, they were giving out some glow and they had 'BB' written on them with a golden colour. Isabell handed them to us and we accepted them.

"Whenever you write with these pens, you'll remember me and your trip to BlossomBliss!" Isabell mentioned.

"We love it," Laura responded.

"Thank you!" Both of us thanked Isabell and she nodded.

That day, we went back home. After having lunch, I took a nap. I was relieved like never before after all that we'd achieved. I made my bed and slept there with that wide smile on my face. It was an adventure; an adventure too memorable for us to remember for the rest of our lives.

THE END